ONE LEAF FELL

By TOBY SPEED

Illustrated by MINERVA McINTYRE

*For Michael and Matthew —
with leafy
good wishes!*

*Toby Speed
Mar. 21, 1996*

STEWART, TABORI & CHANG
NEW YORK

For my children
—T. S.

For my friends Keith and Josie, with special thanks to gracious Ann
—M. M.

ONE LEAF FELL

One leaf fell.

It tumbled down

a hillside and into

a gully.

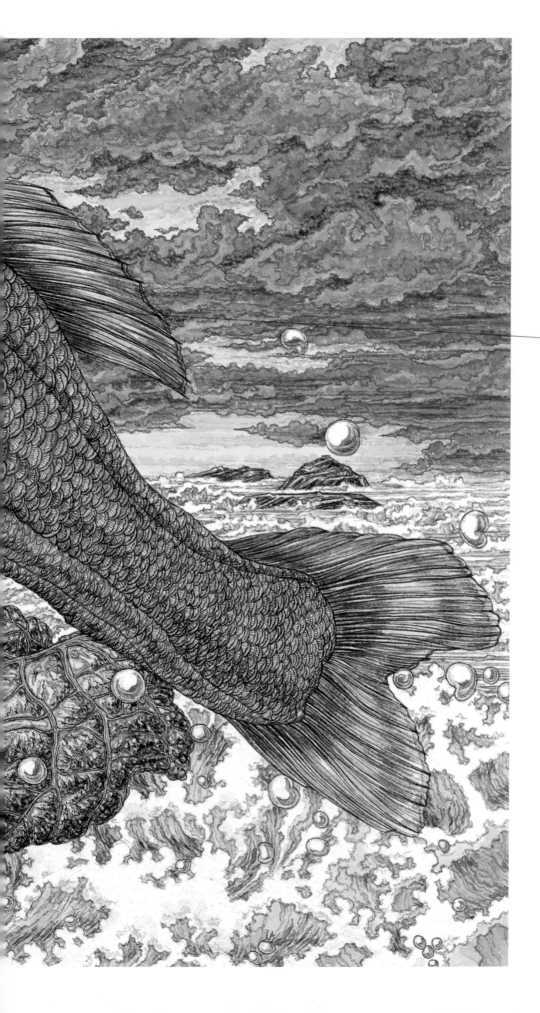

It sailed down

a swift river.

Fish jumped

over it.

Beetles rode on it.

Fallen logs

blocked it.

A horse stopped

to drink from it.

A rabbit hid

under it.

The leaf
cartwheeled past
cornstalks and
into some woods.

It hopped from
limb to limb to
limb, just visiting.
It chased other
leaves and acorns.

After that, the leaf was ready for a good rest, so it curled up beside a tree stump and stayed there all winter.

When the snow melted, a sparrow snatched up the leaf and took it back to use for her nest.

Three baby
sparrows
snuggled up
to it.

Warm rain

and moonlight

washed it.

Crickets sang to it.

Then one day . . .

The sparrows

were gone

and everything

was quiet.

Summer was over.

The tree

shivered in the

cool night air.

One leaf fell.

Text copyright © 1993 Toby Speed
Illustration copyright © 1993 Minerva McIntyre

Designed by Julie Rauer and Amanda Wilson

Published in 1993 by
Stewart, Tabori & Chang
575 Broadway, New York, New York 10012

Library of Congress Cataloging-in-Publication Data

Speed, Toby.
    One leaf fell / by Toby Speed ; illustrated by
    Minerva McIntyre.
        p.   cm.
    Summary: Follows the day-to-day life of a fallen
    leaf as it provides transportation, housing, and other
    services to various animals.
    ISBN 1-55670-271-X
    [1. Leaves—Fiction.   2. Animals—Fiction.
    3. Nature—Fiction.]   I. McIntyre, Minerva, ill.
    II. Title.
    PZ7.S7461150n   1993
    [E]—dc20   92-44942
                                                      CIP

Distributed in the U.S. by
Workman Publishing, 708 Broadway
New York, New York 10003

Distributed in Canada by
Canadian Manda Group, P.O. Box 920
Station U, Toronto, Ontario, M8Z 5P9

Distributed in all other territories by
Melia Publishing Services, P.O. Box 1639
Maidenhead, Berkshire, SL6 6YZ England

First Edition

Composed with QuarkXpress 3.1 on a Macintosh IIsi
in Simoncini Garamond at Stewart, Tabori & Chang,
New York. Output on a Linotronic L300 at
Typogram, Inc., New York.

Printed and bound by
Toppan Printing Company, Ltd., Singapore